Mittie Cuetara

The Crazy Crawler Crane and Other Very Short Truck Stories

Dutton Children's Books      New York

For Mom and Dave and my own little truck lover

CIP Data is available.
Published in the United States 1997 by Dutton Children's Books,
a member of Penguin Putnam Inc.
375 Hudson Street, New York, New York 10014
Designed by Semadar Megged
Printed in Hong Kong
First Edition
10 9 8 7 6 5 4 3 2 1
ISBN 0-525-45951-0

Contents

Garbage Truck • 4

Fire Truck • 6

School Bus • 8

Crawler Crane • 10

Tow Truck • 12

Moving Van • 14

Ambulance • 16

Police Car • 18

Cement Mixer • 20

Cherry Picker • 22

Tractor Trailer • 24

Dump Truck • 26

Excavator • 28

Delivery Vans • 30

GARBAGE TRUCK

A tough metal shell...

strong personnel...

Kids think it's swell,

except for the smell.

FIRE TRUCK

The firefighters all looked tired.

"Was it a bad one?" I inquired.

Oh, yes, as bad as it could be—

a mean old cat in a big, tall tree.

SCHOOL BUS

The driver is having a fit,

trying to get them to sit.

They giggle and wiggle and hit

and don't pay attention one bit.

CRAWLER CRANE

The crawler crane has gone insane.

Oh my gosh, it's grabbing Jane!

Look out, Jane is angry now.

She kicks it in the treads, kapow!

TOW TRUCK

Yak yak!

Ouch, smack!

Bad luck!

Tow truck.

13

MOVING VAN

This van is long and wide

with lots of room inside.

Here's our couch and chandelier.

Why don't we just move in here?

15

Ambulance

Ned was a very sick boy.

He'd swallowed a part of his toy.

The doc fixed him up good as new.

Sorry, the toy won't pull through.

17

Police Car

The cops are on the job   when someone tries to rob.

The culprit is exposed....

Another case is closed.

CEMENT MIXER

Stop and load up with sand.

Go where construction is planned.

Pour out concrete on demand.

Oops. Watch out where you stand.

cherry picker

I love it way up high.

I love the clear blue sky.

That's why I want to be

the one who trims the tree.

Tractor Trailer

Joe sleeps while Jill's at the wheel,

driving the rig loaded with steel.

When they switch, Jill gets to sleep.   Joe counts the miles, as Jill counts sheep.

Dump Truck

I do this job, I do it right.

I work at this construction site.

I work quite hard, as you can see,   considering I'm only three.

exCavator

The yellow beast will crunch and chew

as if he's at a barbecue.

And though it's not polite to do,

he spits his meal out when he's through.

Delivery Vans

Things to sit on, things to wear,

Videos, a Frigidaire.

Things to eat, from cake to liver.

So many things they will deliver.